SCOOBY-DOO!™

WHERE'S SCOOBY?

A search-and-find book

Adapted from 'Look and Find Scooby-Doo' written by Emily Thoton Calvo and Joel Zadak and illustrated by Animagination, Inc. and CaveMan Productions.

Also adapted from 'Look and Find What's New Scooby-Doo' written by Jamie Elder and illustrated by Art Mawhinney.

Published by Scholastic Australia in 2023.
PO Box 579 Gosford NSW 225
ABN 11 000 614 577
www.scholastic.com.au

Part of the Scholastic Group
Sydney • Auckland • New York • Toronto • London • Mexico City • New Delhi • Hong Kong • Buenos Aires • Puerto Rico

ISBN 978-1-76129-747-2

Edited by Imogen Nutting
Cover design by Simone Kelleher

Printed in China.

Scholastic Australia's policy, in association with its printers, is to use papers that are renewable and made efficiently from wood grown in responsibly managed forests, so as to minimise its environmental footprint.

SCHOLASTIC
SYDNEY AUCKLAND NEW YORK TORONTO LONDON MEXICO CITY
NEW DELHI HONG KONG BUENOS AIRES PUERTO RICO

MEET THE GANG!

SCOOBERT (SCOOBY) DOO

This Great Dane may be terrified of ghosts and monsters, but he'll do anything for a Scooby Snack!

NORVILLE (SHAGGY) RODGERS

A laid-back scaredy-cat who would rather look for food than search for clues, but he usually finds both!

DAPHNE BLAKE

The gang's resident fashion queen, Daphne solves her mysteries in style.

VELMA DINKLEY

Velma's a pro at catching crooks and usually puts the missing pieces together to solve the mystery!

FRED JONES

The leader of the gang, Fred's good at setting traps and catching crooks!

THE MYSTERY MACHINE

This van takes the gang from mystery to mystery, offering a safe haven as they run away from (or towards) various monsters.

LOCATIONS

Look out for Scooby and the gang as they travel across the globe to explore some amazing places. In each location, you'll find the gang meeting new people and engaging in different activities. Check pages 34 and 35 for lists of additional characters and objects hidden in the scene.

WATERPARK

JUNGLE

TOY STORE

FUNLAND

MUSEUM

SKI SLOPES

CASTLE

MYSTERY KIDS ROOM

MAGIC SHOW

VOLCANO

BASEBALL

PIRATE COVE

CAMP SITE

THE MYSTERY MACHINE

CAN YOU FIND EVERY SCOOBY?

SCAREDY DOO ☐

MYSTERY DOO ☐

MAGIC SCOOBY ☐

JUNGLE SCOOBY ☐

SLIDING SCOOBY ☐

SNACKY DOO ☐

BASEBALL SCOOBY ☐

ROBO SCOOBY ☐

MUMMY DOO ☐

PIRATE SCOOBY ☐

SCOOBY-DOO-BBQ ☐

ICE SCOOB ☐

SCOOBY DUKE ☐

BONUS!

SCOOBY BOO ☐

THE WATERPARK

The gang is in New Orleans for Mardi Gras, hoping to spot a ghost. Sure enough, in the water park next to the cemetery, two Civil War ghosts, Jed and Caleb Leland, chase after them.

Find Scooby-Doo, Shaggy, Fred, Daphne and Velma and help them escape the Leland Brothers.

CHIPS

MYSTERY KIDS ROOM

The gang finds out that the Mystery Machine once belonged to the Mystery Kids band! When the van starts acting weird, they take it to their mechanic, Murph. At the shop, they find out that Murph has been acting weird, too. In Murph's private office, there is a Mystery Kids shrine.

Look for these Mystery Kids things to help solve the mystery.

Mystery Kids lunch box

Mystery Kids night-light

Mystery Kids record album

Mystery Kids alarm clock

Mystery Kids T-shirt

Mystery Kids lamp

Mystery Kids board game

MK
OIL
OIL
OIL
OIL
OIL
GAME
Bubble Bath
WAS

MAGIC SHOW

The gang goes to Las Vegas to catch a concert, but the ghost of Rufus Raucous is trying to sabotage it. But wait! The real Rufus Raucous is alive and well and sabotages the ghost with his famous tricks. Look for these magical things.

Magic scarf

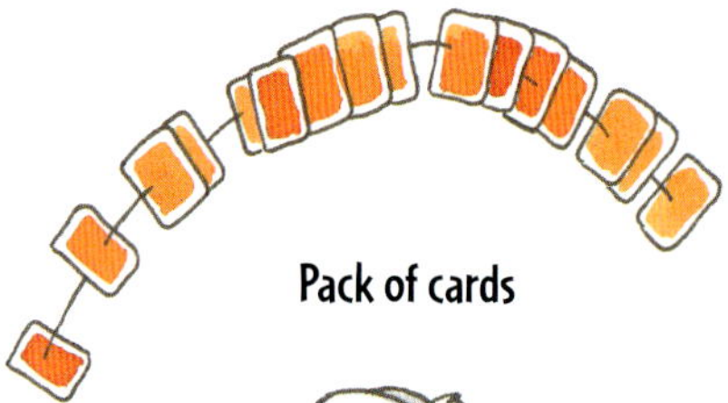

Pack of cards

Top hat

Floating bottle

Dove box

Linking rings

Sword box

HAIR REMOVING CREAM
ANTI-BALDING CREAM
NOSE STRIPS
CAUTION MAGNETIC POLARITY
WHITENING GEL
WRINKLE CREAM
DEEP HEAT

JUNGLE

Scooby-Doo, where are you? All the animals in the jungle have gone ape. They are wild and glowing and Scooby is among them.

Help solve the mystery by looking for these animals in their altered states.

ANIMAL CRACKERS
ANIMAL CRACKERS

TOY STORE

While shopping for a gift, Scooby, Shaggy, Fred, Daphne and Velma find that the toys aren't playing around when they come to life in the toy store.

Stay with the gang after the mall closes and help them uncover the real mystery by finding these strange toys.

Battleship

G.I. Steve

Paratrooper

Jeep

Tank

Soldier

Jet

SALE
SALE
CEMENT
PHONES

VOLCANO

While Scooby and the gang holiday in Italy, they hear about the ghost of a gladiator who lived when Mount Vesuvius erupted the first time in 79 AD. The meddling bambinos go to Pompeii to investigate and discover that the volcano might erupt again!

Help solve the mystery by finding these ancient artifacts in the piles of garbage.

Helmet

Vase

Pot

Candelabra

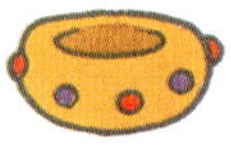

Bracelet

Sculpture

Painting

BASEBALL GAME

The gang wins a contest to meet Luis Santiago, who is trying to break the all-time home run record. After the introductions, they become acquainted with a ghost who throws flaming heat at Luis to keep him from reaching his goal.

Help the gang discover the mystery of the fiery fastballs.

Regular baseballs

Fire extinguisher

Bucket of sand

Matches

Gasoline

Kerosene

Pail of water

SNACKS
PEANUTS
LUIS
GAS
I ♥ LUIS
H
KEROSENE
SANTIAGO
1
ROSIN
BIG BLOW

FUNLAND

Welcome to Funland Amusement Park! Kids had fun here, but now Mr Jenkins' haywire, ghostly robots are up to foul play.

Scooby-Doo and his friends are out to capture the ghostly gadgets, but more than one robot is trying to take them for a ride.

Take a look and see if you can find Scooby-Doo and his amusing pals trying to put the fun back in Funland.

Chip Disk

Scooby-Doo Robo

Robo-Ghost

Heavy Metal

Robo-Mop

R2D2B12

Robo-Bobo the Clown

FERRIS WHEEL'S DAY OFF
ROLLER DERBY COASTER
FORTUNE TELLING
HOT DOGS
BALL TOSS
23

MUSEUM

While at the Museum of Archeology, Scooby and his friends are chased by a ghastly mummy. The monster wants an ancient coin that's the key to unlocking a priceless treasure. The gang needs help to find the coin before the mummy does.

Help unravel the mystery by finding the gold coin and these other characters that have gotten all "wrapped" up in this mystery:

Gold Coin

Mummy Scooby

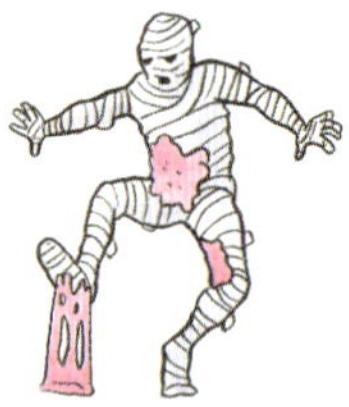
Gummy Mummy

Pharoah Skunk

Mr. Volt

Dr. Dig

Chef Mummy-Mia

Siamese Scaredy-Cat

SNACKS
MAN'S EVOLUTION
HOMO-SCOOBUS
HOMO-ERECTUS
HOMO-CRAWLUS
RAGS TO RICHES
FLOATIN' PHARAOH
MUMMY DEAREST
MUMMIES FOR DUMMIES
DIG 2000

PIRATE SHIP

The ghost of Red Beard and his spooky pirate ship are haunting the sea, and the mystery gang wants to know what's really going on. Through dense fog they find the ship, but where's Red Beard? Zoinks! He pops out of the woodwork—and he's captured Shaggy and Scooby! The ship's creepy crew is hungry and Red Beard wants Shaggy and Scoob to make dinner for them.

Find Scooby then help our fearful heroes find the eerie ingredients of Pirate Stew:

Pirate Scooby

Half a Crow's Nest

Pieces of Eight

A Dash of Pepper

Shivered Timbers

A Barrel of Laughs

A Twist of Lime

A Sprinkle of Gunpowder

SPARE TIRES
FINISH
HOOK'S
ES & SINKERS
CORN: A BUCK AN EAR
Tastes Like Chicken Snack Shop
NIGHT
NLY:
URVY
LOST MARBLES
FOUND MARBLES

CAMP GROUND

Green trees, peaceful lakes, roaring campfires. There's nothing like a camping trip to get away from it all. But it seems that an eerie werewolf has gotten Scooby and the gang wrapped up in yet another mystery. The marshmallows and hot dogs will have to wait until the fearless crew get to the bottom of this hair-raising mystery.

Find the werewolf's treasure map, the creepy werewolf and these other nutty nature buffs:

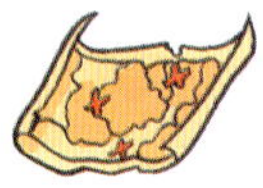

Treasure Map

Grizzly Painter

Timber Buck II

The Werewolf

A Fox in Socks

Forest Stump

Scooby-Doo-BBQ

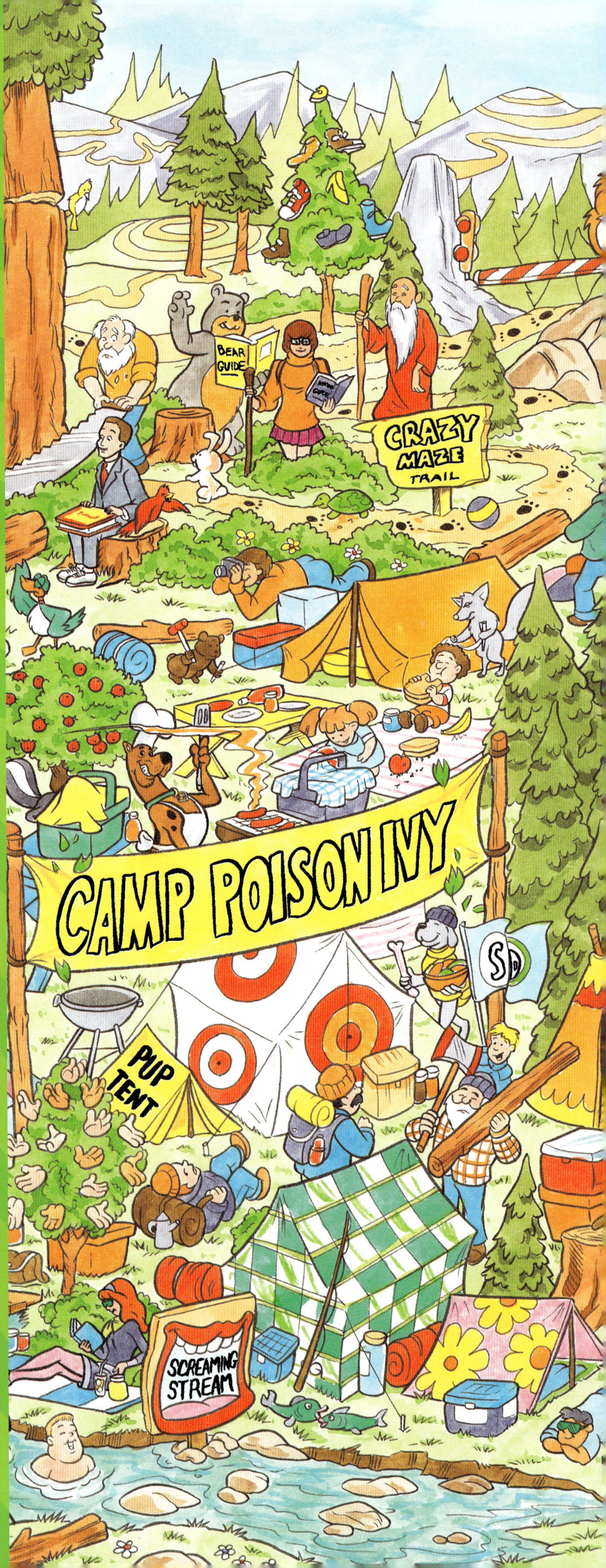

MINE
GET YOUR OWN
OLD MILL
BEAR HUGS 50¢
SILAS LONG
MISTER BONE JANGLES
WASH 'N WEARWOLF
DYED 1980
POISON IVY RELIEF
CONE SWEET CONE
NURSERY

SKI FIELD

Scooby-Doo and the gang head for the mountains on a ski weekend. After hearing about the Yeti Snow Ghost that's been terrorising the area, Scooby-Doo and the gang know there's a mystery to solve!

Ice is not the only thing sparkling on these peaks, there are secret jewels the Snow Ghost doesn't want anyone to find. Help the gang find the jewels, catch the monster, alert the sheriff and try to have some fun on their trip.

Sheriff

Snow Ghost

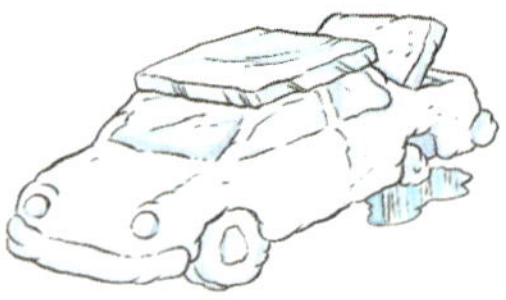
Snowmobile

White Timberwolf

Ice-Scoob

Ghoul's Jewels

Snow Boarder

PEPPER
SNOW TIRES
RESORT TO SKIING
CREEPY SLEEPY LODGE
SANTA SLEPT HERE
LODGE
RESERVATIONS
FROZEN FOOD COURT
SPECIAL: YETTI SPAGETTI
HOG SLED RIDES
SNO GLOBE GIFT SHOP
MELTAWAYS
YETTI PETTYS
BOOKS
ESKIMO PIE
BLUEBERRY AND APPLE
POLAR ROOT BEER
CLIFF'S CLIFF

CASTLE

Scooby-Doo and the gang visit a castle expecting to get the royal treatment. But a freaky phantom is causing a royal pain. The ghastly ghost is looking for a treasure that has been hidden away. And ghosts are everywhere causing the royal blues.

Explore the castle and see if you can find the treasure chest, the phantom and some loyal royals.

Queen Bee
Scooby-Duke
King Crab
Silent Knight
Foot Prince
Royal Jewels
Phantom of the Castle

SWEET SCREAMS
NO PETS ALLOWED
HAUNTED CASTLE MAP
POOL HALL
GHOUL HALL
BLOOD DONORS WELCOME
NO BRIDGE PLAYING

MORE CHARACTERS AND OBJECTS TO SEARCH AND FIND:

Go back to the water park and help Daphne find her spare shoes that were scattered in the chase.

- [ ] True shoe
- [ ] Blue shoe
- [ ] Moo shoe
- [ ] Glue shoe
- [ ] Flew shoe
- [ ] Cuckoo shoe

Go back to the Mystery Kids room and look for evidence of Murph's other hobbies.

- [ ] Coin collection
- [ ] Stamp collection
- [ ] Origami
- [ ] Needlepoint
- [ ] Accordion
- [ ] Golf clubs

Go back to Las Vegas and help Rufus and the gang understand the gravity of the situation by finding these clues.

- [ ] Scooby's collar
- [ ] Fred's keys
- [ ] Shaggy's belt buckle
- [ ] Daphne's compact
- [ ] Velma's watch

Go back to the baseball park, where flaming fastballs are flying, and find these other hot things.

- [ ] Hot dog
- [ ] Hot sauce
- [ ] Jalapeño nachos
- [ ] Fireball candy
- [ ] Hot chocolate
- [ ] Spicy meatball sandwich

Go back to Funland Amusement Park and gather all these amusing tools to keep the rides in gear.

- [ ] Screw 'driver'
- [ ] Monkey Wrench
- [ ] C-Saw
- [ ] Nuts and Bolts
- [ ] Biting bins

Go back to the museum to discover these other Ancient Egyptian inspired things:.

- [ ] Pharaoh's Faucet
- [ ] 'Mummies for Dummies'
- [ ] A Pair of Pyramids
- [ ] Cleopatra's Wig
- [ ] Hippo-glyphics
- [ ] A Scroll on a Stroll

Go back to the jungle and find all the animal crackers that Shaggy has spilled.

- [ ] Lion
- [ ] Giraffe
- [ ] Turtle
- [ ] Bear
- [ ] Elephant
- [ ] Camel

Go back to the mall and find the evidence that the toys are trying to keep secret.

- [ ] A crack
- [ ] A drill
- [ ] A jackhammer
- [ ] A pile of stones
- [ ] A coil of rope
- [ ] A bag of cement

Go back to the volcano and find leftover Italian food that Scooby and Shaggy cannot resist.

- [ ] Spaghetti
- [ ] Linguini
- [ ] Lasagna
- [ ] Ravioli
- [ ] Pizza
- [ ] Cannoli

Once the police arrive to bring Red Beard and his goons to justice, they will need to recover all the stolen valuables. Go back to the spooky shore to find these precious items:

- [ ] Treasure 'Chest'
- [ ] Monkey business
- [ ] Remote controlled pirate
- [ ] Ivory Tower
- [ ] 'Marble' Statue

Go back to the camping trip in the woods. Then branch out to find these very unusual trees:

- [ ] Shoe Tree
- [ ] Family Tree
- [ ] Palm Tree
- [ ] Tree-ring Circus
- [ ] Money Tree
- [ ] Fur Tree

The gang finds out that there's no business like snow business. Go back to their ski weekend to find these snowy things:

- [ ] A Snow Bunny
- [ ] Iced 'T'
- [ ] Frozen fish
- [ ] Snow 'Suit'
- [ ] Snow Cap
- [ ] A Snow Angel

Return to the castle and find all these ghostly characters who are being royal pests:

- [ ] Boo Moon
- [ ] Say 'Boo'
- [ ] Boobeard the Pirate
- [ ] Kanga-boo
- [ ] Boo Bell
- [ ] Boo-tanical Garden

ANSWERS

WATERPARK

MYSTERY KIDS ROOM

MAGIC SHOW

JUNGLE

TOY STORE

VOLCANO

BASEBALL

FUNLAND

MUSEUM

PIRATE COVE

CAMP SITE

SKI SLOPES

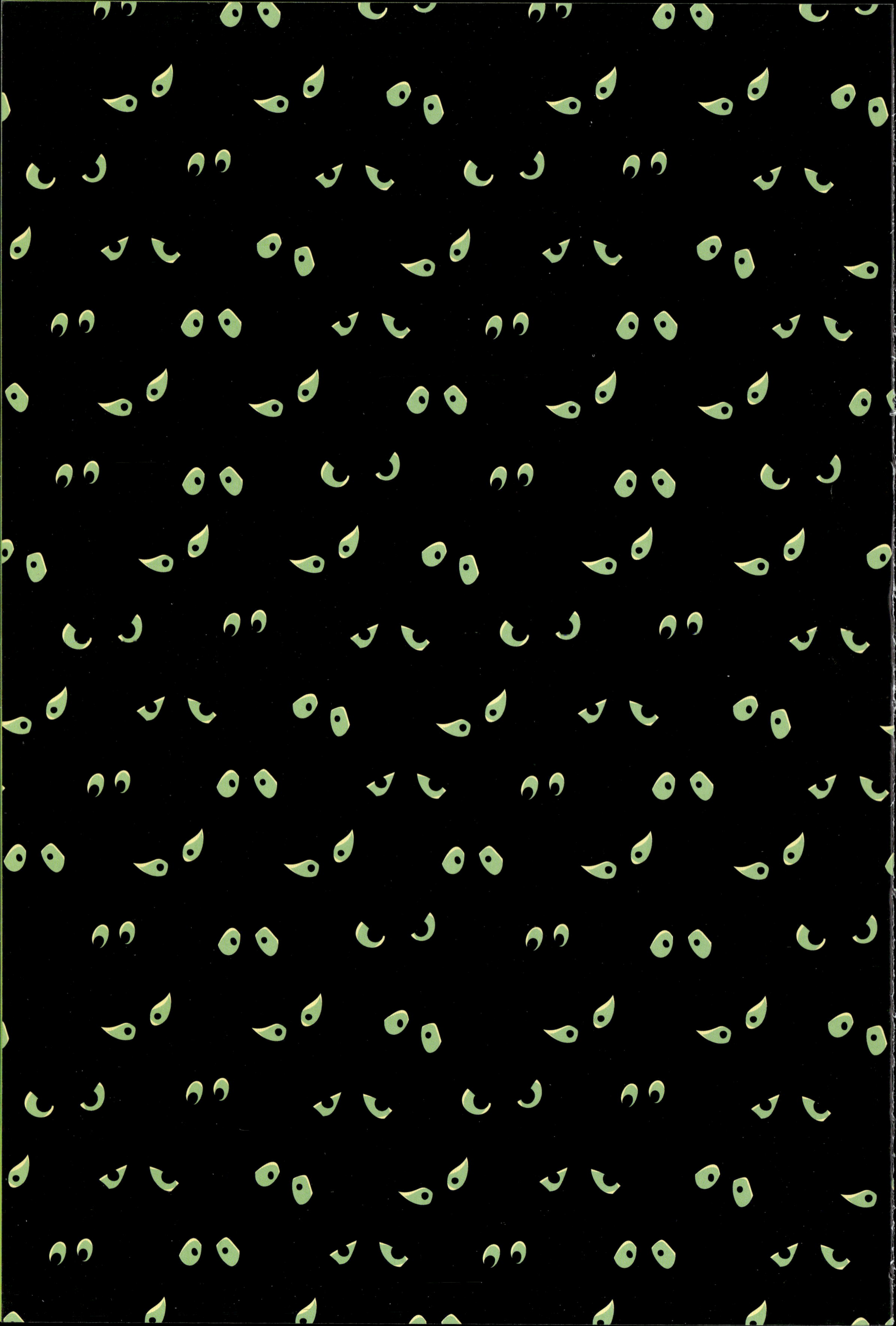